Play It Again, Mallory

For Anna Cavallo—with all my thanks!

And special thanks to Ms. Cathryn Leibinger
for all your help and guidance!
—L.F.

For my mom,
who sacrifices so much to help me
—J.K.

Play It Again, Mallory

by Laurie Friedman

illustrations by Jennifer Kalis

darbycreek
MINNEAPOLIS

CONTENTS

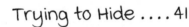

A WORD FROM MALLORY

My name is Mallory McDonald, like the restaurant but no relation, and I'm about to say something I've never said before in my life.

Ready? Here goes . . .

I can't wait for the weekend to end!

You probably think you read that wrong, but you didn't. I can't wait for the weekend to end because I can't wait to go back to school tomorrow.

Now, you're probably thinking I'm crazy or that I ate some poisonous potatoes that were grown to make kids believe they actually want to go back to school. But trust me, I'm not crazy, and I didn't have potatoes this weekend, especially poisonous ones!

6

The reason I want to go back to school tomorrow is that my teacher, Mr. Knight, said that on Monday we're having a special assembly for the Fern Falls fourth, fifth, and sixth graders. He said our principal, Mrs. Finney, has a surprise for us. And I, Mallory McDonald, love, love, love surprises!

My class tried to guess the surprise. We guessed free candy vending machines in school hallways. We guessed movie afternoons. We guessed unlimited recess. We guessed optional math. And we guessed a make-your-own sundae bar in the cafeteria.

Mr. Knight just laughed and said it was none of those things.

Then he said we would have to wait until Monday to hear what Mrs. Finney has to say.

All I have to say is that I can't wait for Monday to get here. I love surprises, and I can't wait to find out what this one is!

AN ASSEMBLY

"Girls and boys, may I have your attention, please," says Mrs. Finney. "The moment you have been waiting for has arrived!"

The Fern Falls Elementary School auditorium is filled with fourth, fifth, and sixth graders. It gets quiet before the teachers even have to ask us to be quiet. Everyone is as excited as I am to hear what Mrs. Finney has to say.

It was hard sitting through math, spelling, and geography this morning. I can hardly wait one more second. The good news is that I don't have to.

Mrs. Finney clears her throat and keeps talking. "This year at Fern Falls Elementary, we are starting a new program called Spring Selections." Mrs. Finney smiles like she's proud of the new program.

"This special program will introduce our fourth, fifth, and sixth graders to the arts that will be offered in middle school. Every one of you will get to choose an arts intensive: band, orchestra, ballet, or drama. You will spend the next six weeks studying your elective. The program will end with the Spring Selections Showcase, a special presentation featuring all the electives. It will be a show for the entire school and all of your parents."

Mrs. Finney pauses like she's waiting for that information to sink in.

Then she continues explaining. "To choose your elective, you will be given a form when you return to your classrooms. Just fill out the form listing your first, second, and third choices, and turn it in to your teachers."

Mrs. Finney pauses again. This time, the auditorium fills up with the sound of kids talking. Everyone around me has something to say.

"This is going to be fun, fun, fun!" says Mary Ann.

"I can't wait to start," says Pamela.

"There are so many things to choose from," says Zoe.

"It's going to be so hard to pick," says April.

"Your attention, please!" says Mrs. Finney.

She raises her hand, which is what she does in assemblies when she wants students to be quiet.

Usually our principal looks mean when her hand goes up, but today she is all smiles.

Portrait of a Principal with Her Hand Up

Most Days! | **Today!**

"Girls and boys, before you leave to go back to your classrooms, I have some special teachers I would like to introduce to you."

She motions backstage, and four adults join her at the podium.

I recognize one of them. Mrs. Denson was the director of *Annie*, the show I was in earlier this year. I'm so happy she's back. She was an awesome director. It might be hard for some people to pick what they want to do, but I already know which elective I'm going to pick. I would love to be in another show directed by Mrs. Denson.

Mrs. Finney keeps talking. "First, I would like to introduce Mr. Todd Michaels, the Fern Falls High School orchestra director. He will be leading the orchestra group, who will learn to play string instruments during Spring Selections."

Mr. Michaels has a beard and glasses and

a friendly face. He tucks a violin under his chin and begins to play. When he's done, he bows and everyone claps.

"Next up is Mrs. Kate Denson. She is the Fern Falls Middle School drama teacher. Some of you already know her from our production of *Annie* that she directed earlier this year."

There's lots of clapping and cheering. Everyone loved Mrs. Denson.

Mrs. Denson starts to sing a song called "There's No Business Like Show Business." When she's done, she waves to the crowd in a dramatic way. I wave back to try to get her attention, but I can't tell if she can see me from up on the stage.

"Next, we have Ms. Brigitte Fontaine. She is a local ballet teacher who moved to the United States from France just last year. She will be teaching the ballet section of Spring Selections."

Everyone claps as Ms. Fontaine leaps and twirls across the stage and then curtsies.

"And last but certainly not least, we have Ms. Katherine Anderson. She is the director of the Fern Falls Middle School Band, and she is very excited to work with elementary students who want to learn to play brass, woodwind, and percussion instruments."

Ms. Anderson is holding an instrument in her hand. She holds it up to her mouth and starts playing a song. "That's a saxophone," Pamela whispers to Joey and me.

When Ms. Anderson is done, everyone claps. She bows to the audience.

"That's so cool," says Joey. "I want to learn to play the saxophone. Spring Selections is going to be awesome!"

I agree, and so does everyone else. There's so much noise in the auditorium that it sounds like we're at a soccer game, not a school assembly.

A bell rings, signaling the assembly is over. "All right, everyone, back to your classrooms," says Mrs. Finney over all the noise.

As we leave the auditorium, everyone is talking about Spring Selections and what they want to do.

"I've always danced hip-hop. I can't wait to try ballet," says Mary Ann.

"We're going to sign up for ballet too," Arielle and Danielle say at the same time.

"I'm excited to play in an orchestra," says Pamela. She has been playing the violin since she was little. "It will be so much fun to play as part of an orchestra with everyone."

"I want to be in the band," says Joey.

"Me too," says Pete. They high-five each other as they walk.

"I can't wait to work with Mrs. Denson again," I say.

Mary Ann does a little skip-dance as we walk back to class. I skip-dance alongside her. Everyone is excited about Spring Selections. Including me.

IT'S NOT FAIR!

"Waiting takes forever!" I say. I squeeze Mary Ann's hand as we walk into the cafeteria. "I don't think I can wait another minute to see what we got!"

The assembly when Mrs. Finney announced Spring Selections was a week ago. After the assembly, we all went back to our classrooms and filled out the Spring Selections forms with our first, second, and third choices.

Today's the day we find out which elective we've been placed into.

I know Mary Ann is just as excited as I am. And so are a lot of other kids. The cafeteria is packed. Everyone is crowded around a big sheet of paper that is posted on the wall.

"C'mon!" says Mary Ann. We push our way to the front. "I'm in ballet!" she screams when she looks at the list.

"Me too!" says Arielle who is standing next to Mary Ann.

"So am I!" screams Danielle.

All three of them start jumping around in a circle like they're super happy. I push past them. I want to see what I'm in. I want to start jumping around in a happy circle too.

But when I see my name on the sheet of paper, I don't start jumping. I start rubbing my eyes to make sure I'm seeing what I think I'm seeing.

I look again, and I see the same thing I saw the first time. My name is listed under the column that says: BAND.

I, Mallory McDonald, who signed up for drama as my first choice, ballet as my second choice, and band as my third choice, got placed into my third choice, BAND!

The next thing I know, lots of kids from my class are jumping around me and screaming that they are so happy because they got what they wanted.

Mary Ann, Arielle, and Danielle got into ballet. Just like they wanted.

Pamela, Zoe, and Jackson got into orchestra. Just like they wanted.

April, Sammy, and Adam got into drama. Just like they wanted.

And Joey, C-Lo, and Grace got into the band. Just like they wanted.

Even my brother, Max, and his best friend, Dylan, got into their first choice, band. And Max's girlfriend, Winnie, got into her first choice, drama.

The noise of everyone talking about what they got swirls around me.

But I'm speechless. I can't believe I
didn't get into my first choice or my second
choice. I got stuck in my third choice, band!

It's *NOT* fair!

And what's completely *NOT* fair is that
I'm one of the few people in my class who
didn't get their first choice. OK. Zack,
Emma, and Evan got put into their second
choices, and Dawn, Nicholas, and Brittany
got placed into their third choices.

But here's the thing . . . Zack, Emma,
Evan, Dawn, Nicholas, and Brittany all say
they don't care what they got.

BUT I DO! I care a lot.

It's *NOT* fair that so many kids got what
they wanted and I didn't.

And I'll tell you what else is NOT fair: the
letter posted on the wall from Mrs. Finney.

It's a very official-looking letter and, if
you ask me, not a very friendly one.

Fern Falls Elementary
A note from Principal Finney

Dear Students:

I hope you are all looking forward to beginning Spring Selections. You were carefully placed into your electives. The administration tried to accommodate all requests. It was simply not possible in all cases. Please note that there will be NO switching between electives.

Rehearsals begin this afternoon.

Good luck and have fun!
Mrs. Finney

Like I said, it's *NOT* fair!

FROM BAD TO AWFUL

I sling my backpack off my back and plop down on the couch. Friday afternoons are a happy time for most people.

Some Friday afternoons, I'm one of those people.

But not this Friday afternoon.

When I went to school Monday morning, I knew my week was starting off badly. I found out I was in band. I wanted to be in drama. The letter from Mrs. Finney said no switching. I didn't think Spring Selections was going to go well for me.

But a lot of my friends were excited, and they thought I should be too.

"It's going to be awesome," said Mary Ann.

"You should be open-minded," said Pamela.

"Give band a try," said Joey.

So I decided I would.

But now that we're one week into Spring Selections, I know it's not going to go well for me. What started off just plain bad on Monday morning went to downright awful this afternoon. I'm talking about the kind of awful where you pinch yourself to see if hopefully you're having a bad dream, but when you look down at your arm, you see a big red mark and you know you're wide awake.

That's exactly the kind of awful that happened to me, and it happened this afternoon during band practice.

It sounds like I'm being dramatic, but trust me, I'm not. If you don't believe me, just keep reading and you'll see what I mean.

MONDAY

It all started Monday afternoon after school. We had our first band practice.

"Welcome!" said Ms. Anderson. She held open the door of room 102 as the members of the Fern Falls Elementary School band entered for our first official practice. When we got inside, there were lots of instruments stacked against the wall. Ms. Anderson went around the room and had students introduce themselves. She smiled a lot and even made a music joke.

Question: What is the loudest pet?
Answer: The trum-pet!

Then she introduced us to the different instruments we would be learning to play. She showed us woodwind, percussion, and brass instruments. We did a listening exercise so we could start to identify the sounds made by different instruments.

"You will get to know the instruments this week, and I will get to know all of you. That way I can match each of you up with an instrument." Ms. Anderson said matching up students with instruments is one of her specialties.

When she said that, I looked at the instruments against the wall. Some of the

instruments I had seen before, and some
I had not. Some looked like they actually
might be fun to play. Some looked like
they might have been invented on another
planet.

Monday afternoon, I crossed my toes
and made a wish that Ms. Anderson would
match me up with the right instrument,
which in my opinion would be one that
would NOT make me look like I'm from
outer space.

The Mars Marching Band

TUESDAY

Tuesday afternoon at band practice was woodwinds day. Ms. Anderson had us take notes about woodwind instruments.

Then she showed us different

Woodwinds

Sound is produced in a woodwind instrument by blowing air into a mouthpiece against a sharp edge or through a reed. Woodwind instruments have holes and keys that the musician covers up or presses to change notes.

woodwind instruments. She showed us flutes, oboes, bassoons, clarinets, and saxophones.

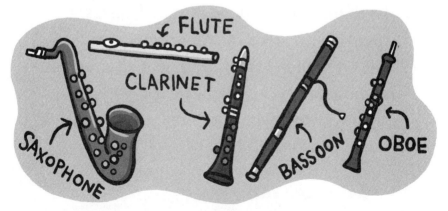

When she was done, she let everyone touch the instruments and even try them. Then she had everyone practice the mouth positions for playing each one. We all looked funny with our mouths moving, but no one seemed to mind. There were so many different woodwind instruments that all made different sounds. Some sounded pretty, like the flute. And some sounded cool, like the saxophone.

Joey said he would love to play the saxophone. A girl in my class, Grace, said she liked the clarinet. Two fifth graders, Jamie and Olivia, said they wanted to play the flute. Olivia's friend, Brianna, said she would like to learn the oboe.

Even though I wanted to be in drama, not band, I could actually hear myself playing a woodwind instrument.

And I liked what I heard.

WEDNESDAY

Wednesday afternoon was percussion day at band practice.

"Sound is made by percussion instruments when two objects are struck together," Ms. Anderson told us.

She showed us the percussion instruments that people would be playing. There were drums, cymbals, and tambourines.

SNARE DRUM

CYMBALS

TAMBOURINE

First, she had everyone do a clapping exercise. Then she introduced all of us to the snare drum. She showed us how to hold the drumsticks and how to use them. Then she demonstrated how cymbals and tambourines are played. It was a lot of fun and very loud! Everyone loved it—especially the boys.

My brother, Max, and his friend Dylan both decided they wanted to play the drums.

I said I might want to be a drummer too. It was a lot of fun playing the snare drum. But Max said we didn't need to be the McDonald family drummers, so I said that I might want to play the cymbals instead.

On the way home from practice, I told Joey that I thought it would be fun to play the cymbals.

He agreed, and he said it would be *really* fun to play the cymbals in the morning in Max's room while he was still sleeping.

I told Joey that sounded like *tons* of fun.

This is your wake-up call!

THURSDAY

Thursday afternoon was brass day in band. Ms. Anderson introduced us to trumpets, trombones, and the tuba.

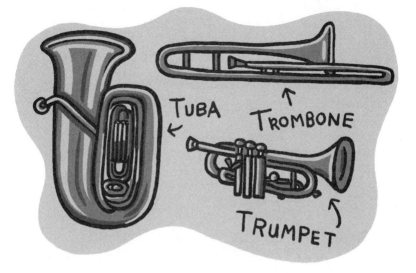

Some of the brass instruments were big. It seemed hard to figure out how to hold them. They looked weird too. When we did mouth exercises for brass mouthpieces, everyone looked even funnier than when we did the woodwind mouthpiece exercises. Lots of people couldn't keep buzzing their lips like we were supposed to because they were laughing too hard. Plus, it just sounded like everyone had a bad case of gas.

Ms. Anderson had us write down some facts about brass instruments.

BRASS

Brass instruments are made from brass or another metal. Sound is produced through vibration of the lips on a mouthpiece. Changing the length of a sound tube with a valve or slide changes the note being played.

But when I reread what I wrote, I had no idea what it meant. The only place I had ever heard of a slide was on the playground.

To me, the brass instruments didn't sound pretty like some of the woodwinds. And they didn't seem fun to play like some of the percussion instruments.

When we were done trying out all the instruments, Ms. Anderson said she would let us all know on Friday which instruments we would be playing.

When I went to bed Thursday night, I made a wish that Ms. Anderson would cross me off the brass instrument list.

Then I went to sleep.

FRIDAY

Now, it's Friday. Remember when I told you that Friday was when my week went from just-plain bad to downright awful? Well, today was that day. It all happened this afternoon at band practice when Ms. Anderson assigned instruments.

Before she assigned them, she said a lot of stuff about how not everyone can play the same instrument, but each instrument can be fun and challenging.

Then she said more stuff about how she has to consider a lot of factors like physical characteristics and personality and musical strengths. And then she started reading the list of who would be playing what.

Max and Dylan were both playing the drums.

Joey and a fifth grader, Yvette, were playing saxophone.

Grace was playing the clarinet.

Ms. Anderson read off lots of names and paired kids up with lots of instruments. I waited until I heard my name. And when I did, I almost fainted.

"Mallory McDonald and Calvin Strong will be playing tuba," said Ms. Anderson.

At first, I thought she was joking. But when Ms. Anderson set a giant black tuba case in front of me, I knew it was no joke.

I couldn't believe it. I could NOT picture myself playing the tuba.

When Ms. Anderson finished reading the list of who would be playing which instruments, she said we would be starting to learn to read music and play our instruments on Monday. "You'll start taking your instruments home next week!"

Before class was over, she gave us all booklets about our instruments and said we should read them over the weekend and get to know our instruments. "Have a happy weekend," she said as we left.

But I couldn't see how my weekend would possibly be happy.

First, I got put in band. Now I'm supposed to get to know the tuba, which I never wanted to play in the first place.

See what I meant when I said my week went from bad to awful?

TRYING TO HIDE

"I can't believe Spring Selections Showcase is in five weeks!" Mary Ann pirouettes as she says it. Then she does an arabesque. Then she curtsies. All while we're walking to school!

"How do you like my ballet moves?" she asks.

She doesn't even wait for me to answer. "We're starting to learn our dance for the show this week," says Mary Ann. She does a series of leaps down the sidewalk.

"Great!" I fake a smile so I look like I'm happy, but I'm not.

I can tell Mary Ann is excited to start practicing her dance in ballet. I wish I could say the same thing about band.

We started practicing on our instruments' mouthpieces yesterday, and I'm NOT happy about playing the tuba or its mouthpiece in earshot of anyone else. It has been all I can think about.

When I tried practicing with the mouthpiece at home yesterday, Max told me I should lay off the beans. I know he thought he was being funny, but I didn't find it so hilarious.

Mom had something to say too, but luckily not about beans.

She said I should really give the tuba a chance. She reminded me that the reason I never liked playing the piano is because I never really tried to learn. I reminded Mom that even though she's a music teacher, it doesn't mean that I'll like playing an instrument.

Mom said I just need to be open-minded and give the tuba a fair chance.

As Mary Ann and I walk into our classroom, I make a wish that the day will pass by slowly. But the morning flies by. While I should be thinking about math, spelling, and geography, my brain keeps thinking about playing the tuba this afternoon at band practice.

At lunch, Spring Selections is what everyone is talking about.

"We practiced ballet all weekend and last night," says Arielle.

Danielle nods like what Arielle is saying is true. "We're so excited to start learning our dance for the showcase. We're going to practice every night at home," she tells Mary Ann.

"I'm going to do that too!" says Mary Ann.

She and Arielle and Danielle high-five each other like they're super excited to practice ballet.

"We're starting our piece in drama for the showcase today too," says April. She takes a bite of her apple, then puts it down on her tray. "I'm so excited, I can hardly eat.

Mrs. Denson is so nice, and drama is so much fun."

"In orchestra, we're going to start learning to play our instruments," says Pamela. Then she tells everyone at the table that since she has already taken violin lessons, Mr. Michaels said she could start learning the piece for the show.

I try not to listen while they all keep talking about how excited they are about Spring Selections. But it's impossible. It's the only thing anyone is talking about.

When we get back to our classroom after lunch, I look at the clock and make another wish that the afternoon will pass more slowly than the morning. But my wish does not come true. Before I know it, I'm in the band room with all the other band members.

"Good afternoon, boys and girls." Ms. Anderson is as cheery as ever. "Today, you will learn how to properly hold your instruments, and we will start playing."

She goes around the room, helping everyone get into position.

Some kids have an easier time than others. Especially the kids with smaller instruments like flutes and oboes.

Jamie and Olivia, two girls in fifth grade who are both playing the flute, have no problems at all. Dawn, in my class, is playing the clarinet. A sixth-grade boy, Brett, is playing the bassoon, and Joey and a fifth grader, Yvette, are playing saxophones.

"Good job!" says Ms. Anderson when everyone in the woodwind section is settled in.

Then she helps the percussionists.

Max and his friend Dylan don't have any problem getting comfortable behind their drums. They both pick up their sticks and start beating their snare drums.

"I feel like a rock star," says Max.

"Me too," says Dylan

Ms. Anderson puts her hands over her ears, but she does it in a nice way, like the sound wasn't quite what it should be, but that's to be expected at the beginning. "Imagine how you'll feel when you learn to play," she says with a smile.

My friend Pete, who is playing the cymbals, picks them up and bangs them together.

It sounds like someone just dropped a big stack of dishes. We all put our hands over our ears. But Pete doesn't look like it bothers him. He bangs his cymbals together again.

"Those are called crash cymbals," says Ms. Anderson. She tells Pete she likes his enthusiasm, but he needs to wait to learn to play the cymbals properly or he'll cause all of us hearing damage. Pete says he wouldn't want to hear of that happening. Ms. Anderson smiles at his joke.

When the percussionists are all settled with their instruments, Ms. Anderson turns her attention to the brass section of the band.

First, she helps Nicholas and Emma, two kids in my class who are both playing the trumpet. The trombone players are next, including C-Lo. When he gets situated, he blows into the mouthpiece of the trombone. His face turns red when he blows. A few kids laugh, but C-Lo doesn't seem to care.

Ms. Anderson tells C-Lo that his tone is not bad and that he has long arms, which are a good thing for trombone players. "I'm sure you'll learn to play quickly," she tells him.

Then Ms. Anderson turns her attention to Calvin and me. She shows us both how to sit and hold our tubas. Calvin seems comfortable with his, but I feel like someone just stuck a huge suitcase on my lap. Ms. Anderson adjusts my back and head and repositions the tuba. When she's satisfied with how we're holding our tubas, she has us blow into the mouthpiece.

Calvin goes first. When he blows into his tuba, it makes a low sound. A few kids laugh.

Even Calvin smiles like he gets how it could be funny.

Ms. Anderson nods like she approves of his first effort. Then she looks at me like I should start. I don't want to do this, but I know I don't have a choice.

I put my lips on the mouthpiece of my tuba, kind of puckering like we tried with our mouthpieces yesterday. But when I blow, a sound comes out that is not a sound anyone would want to make in public. **EVER!**

Everyone is laughing. I can feel my face turning red. I can't help but think of Max's bean jokes. Some of the boys hold their noses like the room stinks.

"Say excuse me," Pete says to my tuba, giggling.

Even Ms. Anderson looks like she's trying not to smile.

"Don't worry, Mallory, the tuba is one of the most important instruments in the band and it will sound much better with practice."

There's more laughter and nose holding.

My face must be as red as a tomato. The tuba might be one of the most important instruments in the band, but it is **NOT** an instrument that I want to learn to play.

Right now, the only thing I want to do with this tuba is hide behind it.

PRACTICE PROBLEMS

It's Saturday morning. I look at the clock beside my bed.

My favorite TV show, *Fashion Fran*, starts in fifteen minutes. It also happens to be my best friend's favorite TV show. We watch it together every Saturday morning.

I walk to the kitchen and call Mary Ann. "Get over here, quick! *Fran* starts in fifteen!" I say when she answers.

"I can't watch today," says Mary Ann. "Arielle and Danielle are coming over to practice our dance for the Spring Selections Showcase."

I can't believe Mary Ann isn't coming over. I open my mouth to convince her, but she keeps talking.

"The show is in four weeks, and everyone I know is busy practicing," says Mary Ann. "You should practice today too. That's what everyone is doing at my house. Joey has been playing the saxophone all morning. Winnie's friends are coming over after lunch to rehearse their parts for the drama presentation."

I blow a piece of hair off my face while Mary Ann is talking. Even though she's my best friend, sometimes I don't like what she has to say. And this is one of those times.

"I'm going to practice later," I tell Mary Ann when she's done talking.

Right now, I'm going to watch my favorite show. Even if I have to watch it by myself.

I make some toast and orange juice and take it in the living room. I turn on the TV.

When I see Fran on the screen, I take a bite of toast and settle in on the couch. Watching my favorite show, even by myself, is more fun than practicing the tuba.

I try to listen to what Fran is saying as she models a colorful skirt and tank top. But I can't hear a thing. There's too much noise coming from the back of the house.

Drum noise! Max can't practice while I'm watching TV.

I march down the hall to Max's room and bang on his door. "Can you practice another time?" I yell over the noise. "I'm trying to watch my favorite show."

I wait for my brother to open the door, but someone else opens the door, and that someone is Mom. "I was listening to your brother practice," she says. "And when I'm done, I will come to your room and listen to you practice. Start getting ready, and I will be there in a few minutes."

She closes the door like the conversation is over.

I take a deep breath as I walk down the hall to my room.

It's Saturday morning. I'm supposed to be watching my favorite TV show. Instead, I've got practice problems.

I'm not talking about the kind you find in the back of your math book. I'm talking about the kind you have when you're supposed to be practicing a musical instrument, and you haven't been.

Ms. Anderson told everyone that we should be practicing at home at least twenty minutes a day. She's been spending a lot of time in band teaching everyone how to read music and count notes.

She even gave us a computer program that we're supposed to use at home when we practice. It records what you play so you can play it back and hear how you sound.

The problem is that when I play, I sound terrible, so I don't like to play.

I look at the tuba sitting in the corner of my room.

Even though Mom is the music teacher at my school, I don't think a music teacher would want to listen to someone play an instrument when it sounds terrible. I'm sure Mom will understand when I tell her I can't play the tuba for her or for anyone else. But just in case she doesn't, I sit down at my desk and start writing.

When Mom comes into my room, I hand her a sheet of paper. She sits down on my bed and starts reading.

10 Reasons Why I, Mallory McDonald, CANNOT PLAY THE TUBA!

Reason #1: I stink at playing the tuba. When I do things I stink at, I lose self-esteem. (Do you want me to be a child with low self-esteem?)

Reason #2: When I play the tuba, it makes a bad sound, which makes me a noise polluter. (Do you want me to be a noise polluter?)

Reason #3: I can't do schoolwork when I'm playing the tuba. If I play the tuba, I might have to repeat fourth grade. (Do you want me to be a fourth-grade repeater?)

Reason #4: It hurts my ears when I play the tuba. (Don't you care about my ears?)

Reason #5: It hurts my cat's ears when I play the tuba. (Don't you care about my cat's ears?)

Reason #6: It will hurt your ears if I play the tuba. (Don't you care about your own ears?)

Reason #7: There are other more fun things I would rather be doing. (For example, watching TV, painting my nails, chewing gum, and coming up with new hairstyles. NOTE: I have come up with 63 new hairstyles this week. What if I come up with one that makes me rich and famous? Don't you want me to be rich and famous?)

Reason #8: There are other less fun things I would rather be doing (like cleaning up my room).

Reason #9: I WANT TO CLEAN UP MY ROOM! (I bet you never thought you'd hear me say this!) I can't do it if I'm playing the tuba!

Reason #10: I don't like playing the tuba. If you make me do something I don't like, how do you think that will make me feel? (The answer, in case you do not know, is bad. VERY, VERY BAD! Is that how you want your only daughter to feel?)

When Mom finishes reading my list, she puts it down on my bed.

I wait for her to say she understands why I can't play the tuba and that I don't have to play it again. Ever. But that's not what she says.

"Mallory, have you ever heard the expression "Practice makes perfect"?

Before I have a chance to say if I've heard it or not, Mom keeps talking.

"The only way for you to improve is to practice. The more you practice, the better you will sound. The better you sound, the more you will like playing. The more you like playing, the more you will want to play."

When Mom finishes her speech, she points to the tuba sitting in the corner of my room. "Mallory Louise McDonald, it is time for you to practice," she says.

Then she leaves my room.

I curl up on my bed and pull Cheeseburger toward me. "I wish I had a fairy godmother who would magically appear and put a spell on me that would instantly make me an amazing tuba player," I mumble to my cat.

I rub the space between her ears and look around my room.

No sign of a fairy godmother anywhere.

HITTING THE WRONG NOTES

"Welcome, boys and girls," says Ms. Anderson. "Mallory, please close the door behind you." She gives me an *I-would-like-to-see-you-NOT-always-be-the-last-to-arrive* look.

I wouldn't always be the last to arrive if band was a place that I was excited to go. But the truth is that I don't like going to band. The reason I don't like going is because I'm always hitting the wrong notes.

I've been practicing.

Maybe not as much as Max, who is always playing his drums, or Joey, who hasn't put his saxophone down since he got it. But no matter what I do, my tuba doesn't make a sound that anyone would want to hear. Spring Selections is just three weeks away, and Ms. Anderson is still correcting my mistakes and always saying the same thing to me: "Play it again, Mallory."

Ms. Anderson clears her throat. "Over the past few weeks, we have discussed lots of musical terms. Today, we are going to have a little music quiz to see how much you remember." Ms. Anderson walks around the room and gives everyone a copy of her music quiz.

Even though I don't usually like quizzes, I like them better than playing the tuba.

When Ms. Anderson gives me my quiz, I take out a pencil and start circling answers.

When everyone is done, she collects the quizzes.

"Rehearsal time," she says in a cheery voice.

We all get our instruments.

"You have all been learning to play your individual instruments," says Ms. Anderson. "Today, we will begin to rehearse the piece for Spring Selections Showcase together by sections."

I try to swallow, but I can't.

Playing the tuba by myself has been bad enough. When Ms. Anderson has been working with the tubas, Calvin has been the only one who heard her correct me. I don't want to play in front of the other brass instrument players. Everyone is going to know that I am a terrible tuba player.

I pretend like I'm at the wish pond on my street, squeeze my eyes shut, and make a wish.

I wish I could be anywhere but here right now.

I open my eyes, but when I do, I'm still sitting in my chair in band class at Fern Falls Elementary.

"Boys and girls, please get out your sheet music," says Ms. Anderson.

I take out the sheet music to "Twinkle, Twinkle, Little Star," the song the band is playing at the Spring Selections Showcase, and prop it up on my music stand.

When we have our music in front of us, Ms. Anderson signals for us to begin.

I try to focus on the notes as I play. There is a lot of squeaking and squawking. Fortunately, I'm not the only one who is making the squeaks and squawks.

"Not bad," says Ms. Anderson. She goes from student to student, helping people make adjustments with their instruments.

When she's done, she addresses the whole group. "The goal is to blend all the instruments together and form a pleasing sound. Let's try it again."

This time, when we play, there is slightly less squeaking and squawking. Some instruments still stick out a little, but there's one that sticks out a lot, and that one is mine.

"Mallory, let's see what we can do to help you," Ms. Anderson says gently. She walks over to my chair and starts making some marks on my sheet music with her pencil. She reminds me to breathe deeply. "Tuba playing takes guts!" she says with a smile. Ms. Anderson gives me an encouraging look.

I nod like I get it. And I do. Ms. Anderson has told me many times that my breath needs to come from my belly, not just my mouth. But what I don't get is why I keep hitting the wrong notes.

I want to get this right. Lots of kids are looking at me. I can feel my face getting hot.

The other tuba player, Calvin, looks at me like he feels sorry for me. "Maybe there's something wrong with your tuba," he says.

I look down at my tuba. I wish that was the problem, but I don't think it is.

"Hey," says Calvin. "Want to hear a tuba joke?"

I can tell I don't have a choice.

"How do you fix a broken tuba?" asks Calvin.

I shake my head. I'm not sure I want to hear the answer.

"With a tuba glue."

Calvin laughs. "Ha-ha! Get it?"

I smile like I think his joke is funny. But to be honest, right now I don't see the humor in any of this.

A PEP TALK

When I open my eyes, I look at the clock beside my bed.

It's 4:19 A.M. It's dark outside, and everyone else in my house is sound asleep. I try to go back to sleep, but I can't. My body feels tired, but my brain is wide awake. It's busy thinking, and the thing it's thinking about is what happened today in band practice.

When we got to practice, Ms. Anderson had us warm up. Then the entire band rehearsed the song for the Spring Selections Showcase together. And unfortunately, my tuba sounded like it was playing a completely different song from all the other instruments. A terrible song.

Ms. Anderson came over to me and told me what I should be doing differently.

But today, Ms. Anderson wasn't the only one who said something.

"Mallory, try opening your eyes when you play so you can read the music," a fifth grader, Frankie, whispered.

"Maybe she needs glasses," mumbled his friend Bennett.

I tried to ignore them, but it was impossible. I know my tuba playing doesn't sound the way it is supposed to sound. I also know I don't want to be the person in the band who ruins the Spring Selections Showcase. But I feel like I'm going to be.

And I don't know how I can improve.
What I'm having is a *T.T.E.* That's short
for *Terrible Tuba Emergency*. I need to talk
to someone, and that someone is asleep

upstairs. I know 4:19 A.M. is not the best time for a talk, but I get out of bed, slip my feet into my fuzzy duck slippers, and walk upstairs to my parents' room.

"Mom," I say shaking her shoulder. "I need to talk to you."

Mom sits up in bed and turns the light on. She looks surprised to see me and so does Dad. I sit down next to my mom. I tell her that I can't sleep because I'm not ready for the showcase, and I don't think there is anything I can do to get ready.

When I'm done talking, Mom looks at me for a minute like she's trying to decide what to say.

"Mallory, you have almost two weeks to go until showtime. If I were you, I would spend every spare minute practicing. If you do, I'm sure you'll be ready."

I shake my head. "I'm not so sure," I tell

Mom. "I've tried practicing, but I'm just not good at playing the tuba."

Mom tucks a piece of hair behind one of my ears. "It takes a lot of practicing to get good." Then she pauses. "It also takes the right kind of practicing. I'm glad you came to talk to me, but I think the person you need to talk to is Ms. Anderson. I'm sure she will have some advice for how to make your practicing more helpful."

I shrug like I'm not sure, but Mom seems like she thinks Ms. Anderson can help. "Sweet potato, get some sleep and go talk to Ms. Anderson tomorrow."

I nod my head that I'll do that. And I will. I don't know what else to do.

The next day, when it's finally time for rehearsal, I go straight to the band room. I get there before anyone else arrives.

Ms. Anderson is already there, setting up the room for rehearsal. When I walk in, she looks up. "Mallory, you're early," she says.

I know she's surprised to see me here first.

"May I talk to you?" I ask quietly.

Ms. Anderson sits and pats a chair beside her like she's been waiting for someone to sit in it.

I sit down and take a deep breath.

"The Spring Selections Showcase is two weeks away. I really want to do a good job, but I'm nowhere near ready. It seems like everyone but me has gotten good at playing an instrument."

I look down at my hands. What I have to say next is the tough part. "I feel like everyone else is going to do a good job onstage." I don't want to start crying in front of Ms. Anderson, but I feel like I'm about to. I clear my throat and keep talking. "I don't want to be the one who messes up the show."

Ms. Anderson nods like she understands exactly what I'm feeling. She smiles in a nice way. I can tell she doesn't want me to be upset.

"Mallory, I'm glad you came to talk to me. Learning an instrument can be really challenging. You're not the first student I've taught that has struggled. I have two things to give you."

"Presents?" I ask.

Ms. Anderson laughs. "I wouldn't exactly call them presents," says Ms. Anderson. "But I hope they will be helpful."

I nod as Ms. Anderson starts writing.

The first thing she gives me is a practice schedule. It has practice time each day split into lip-buzzing exercises, rhythm and breathing exercises, scales, and the concert piece.

"Mallory," says Ms. Anderson, "you're going to need to follow this schedule and practice every day between now and the Spring Selections Showcase. I also want you to come to band practice a few minutes early each day, and I will work with you to make sure you are using the proper technique."

I nod.

"I'm glad to hear that you want to improve," says Ms. Anderson.

Then she looks at me in a sweet way like she's my grandmother, even though she's not related to me or even old. "Mallory, the next thing I'd like to give you is a pep talk."

I listen carefully while Ms. Anderson talks.

"Mallory, being a musician takes dedication, commitment, and a lot of hard work. The process of learning isn't always fun, but I can promise you that the feeling of mastering your instrument and playing it well will be worth all of the hard work."

Ms. Anderson smiles. "I also know that you can do it." She pauses. "I have absolutely no doubt that you, Mallory McDonald, can be a star tuba player."

I give Ms. Anderson an *I'm-not-sure-I'm-the-kind-of-player-who-will-ever-twinkle* look.

Ms. Anderson wraps an arm around me and gives me a big, warm hug. "I will let you in on one of my band director's secrets." She leans in close like she doesn't want anyone else to hear what she's about to say, even though there's no one else in the room.

"There's a little something I call music magic. It's what happens when a musician is paired up with the right instrument. Together, they make magical musical sounds."

She pauses and looks at me. Then she continues. "One of the things I am most proud of is my ability to match up musicians and their instruments. I never would have given the tuba to you if I didn't think you could play it. I promise if you give it a chance and work hard, you and the tuba can make magical musical sounds together."

Part of me thinks Ms. Anderson is more confident in her matchmaking abilities than she should be. But another part of me wants to believe she knows exactly what she's talking about.

"Mallory, you can do this."

I nod. "Thank you, Ms. Anderson. I'm going to do my best." As I say that, the door opens and other members of the band start to come in for rehearsal.

Ms. Anderson smiles at me. "No time like the present to get started," she says.

I pick up my tuba and start warming up.

THE LIFE OF A MUSICIAN

By Mallory McDonald (tuba player)

Once upon a time, there was a sweet, cute girl with red hair and freckles who was going to be playing the tuba in a show at her school.

But there was a problem. The show was less than two weeks away, and the girl wasn't very good at playing the tuba.

She wanted to be good, but she wasn't.

The truth is . . . she had spent a lot of time when she should have been learning to play her tuba and getting ready for the show doing other things like painting her nails, chewing gum, and coming up with new hairstyles (sixty-three of them, to be exact).

Now, she had a lot to do and not much time to do it.

As her teacher said, "This will require dedication, commitment, and hard work. If you want to do this, you must give it everything you've got!"

So the little girl decided to give it everything she had.

She committed herself to learning and practicing the tuba in every spare minute of her time. She decided to become a real musician. But as she soon found out, the life of a musician is a hard one. It is a life filled with challenges.

Challenge #1: Fatigue

Fatigue is a fancy word for being overly tired, and it is what happens when you wake up early (in this case 6:45 A.M. when your usual wake-up time is 7:15 A.M.) and go to bed late (9:30 P.M. when you usually go to bed at 9 P.M.) so that you have extra time to practice your tuba. It is also what happens when you have to lug your *not-so-light* tuba from your room to the garage to practice just so you don't wake up or disturb other people in the house who might be sleeping.

Girl Experiencing fatigue

Challenge #2: Hunger

This is not a fancy word. It is a word everyone knows, and it is what happens when you try to eat your lunch but can't because everyone at your lunch table is making you too sick to eat. This happens when all the people at your table are talking about is how ready they are for the show, and that makes you feel too sick to eat (even Oreos, which are your favorite lunch food) because you know you are NOT ready for the show.

Challenge #3: Stress

This is a mental phenomenon that occurs when your life is a mess and you feel like it is about to get even messier. (Example: You are in a show. You are not ready for the show. You feel like you are the only person who is not ready for the show.

You believe you will single-handedly ruin the entire thing and everyone else in the show will be mad at you.) Stress can cause serious side-effects. I will use this word in a sentence so you can see what I mean. Here goes: I (that means me) am going to ruin an entire show, so I am feeling a LOT of stress!!! I am going to draw a picture so you can get an even clearer idea of what I mean.

GiRL experiencing EXTREME stress AND SERIOUS side-effects

Challenge #4: Body Ache

This is a physical problem that occurs from spending time playing an instrument that is bigger than a small suitcase and probably only a little smaller than the state of Texas. And by body ache, I mean backache, arm ache, neck ache, and even finger ache. Another physical problem that goes with playing the tuba is that you have to blow into it if you want sound to come out of it, so in addition to the aches listed above, mouth ache, jaw ache, tongue ache, and possibly toothache can result. Oh yeah— you also have to listen to yourself play this instrument, so if you don't play it well, the result is earache, which leads to headache.

Challenge #5: Broken Relationships

This is what happens when you try to play an instrument that you are not good at and the people you love (and who are supposed to love you back) get sick of listening to you play. Here is part of a conversation to show you what I mean.

My brother, Max: If I hear you play that thing one more time, I'm going to dump you and your tuba in a nearby river.

Challenge #6: Resentment

Of all the challenges that arise as a result of trying to lead the life of a musician, this one is the worst. It is what happens when you spend so much time doing one thing, to hopefully (but maybe not) get good at it, that you start to resent the very thing you are spending time trying to get good at. You start to think about all the other things in life that you could do and that you might be very good at. For example, I have always wanted to learn to make fancy chocolates. I think I could be a very good fancy chocolate maker.

So, as you can see, the life of a musician is not easy.

It is filled with challenges.

Lots of them.

The End.

P.S. If after reading this story you feel sorry for the sweet, cute girl with red hair and freckles who was faced with many challenges while trying so hard to become a good tuba player, feel free to send donations to her attention at 17 Wish Pond Road. Cash, nail polish, stickers, and hair thingies accepted.

DRESS REHEARSAL

The Fern Falls Elementary School auditorium is filled with dancers, actors, and musicians. Everyone is wearing costumes. The musicians have their instruments. The drama troupe has their props. The ballerinas are in tutus.

It almost seems like tonight is show night, but it's not. It's the dress rehearsal.

Ms. Anderson said in our final practice

this afternoon that we should not be nervous about tonight. She said dress rehearsal is the time to work out all the final kinks so the show goes off without a hitch.

But I can't help feeling a little nervous. I would like for dress rehearsal to go off without a hitch, particularly any hitches from the tuba section. I have been practicing hard since my talk with Ms. Anderson. I cross my toes. I just hope I'm ready.

"Places!" Mrs. Denson says from the microphone.

Since she's the drama teacher, she's in charge of putting the show together.

I gather with the rest of the band members in our area onstage.

"Quiet, please!" says Mrs. Denson.

She waits while everyone settles down. Then she continues.

"Tomorrow night, I will welcome the audience and give the introduction. When I do, the curtain will rise and you will all do the opening number together. Let's go ahead and sing it now, and then you will all go to your designated areas backstage and wait for your turn to perform."

Mrs. Denson counts to three. There's a pianist onstage who starts to play. Mrs. Denson motions for everyone onstage to begin singing the group song.

All the members of the band, the orchestra, the ballerinas, and the drama group sing together. A few people are singing the wrong notes, and Mrs. Denson makes us do it again.

The second time, we get it right.

When we're done, Mrs. Denson shows us how she wants us to exit the stage and return to our designated areas backstage.

When the stage has cleared, she calls the orchestra onstage. Mr. Michaels introduces his musicians.

I listen backstage as they play their song. I'm surprised by how good the orchestra sounds. When they're done, Mr. Michaels tells them he is proud of them.

They return backstage, and Mrs. Denson calls up the ballerinas.

When they go onstage, Ms. Fontaine introduces them. They go through their performance. Ms. Fontaine says it is good, but she wants them to do it one more time. When they finish, I hear Ms. Fontaine clapping and congratulating them. "You will be marvelous tomorrow night," she says with a French accent.

When the ballerinas are done, Mrs. Denson calls up her drama troupe.

As they go onstage, I feel like my stomach

is doing flip-flops. I was a little nervous when we started the dress rehearsal. But now, I am a LOT nervous. The band is next, after the drama troupe. I squeeze my eyes shut and make a wish.

I wish I will do a good job during dress rehearsal.

I really hope my wish comes true. I know the band is ready. I just hope I am too. I've definitely improved in rehearsals. But being onstage feels totally different. I try to take a deep breath as Mrs. Denson tells the drama troupe to start their performance. It only takes one run-through.

"Excellent job!" I hear Mrs. Denson say in her loud, clear director's voice.

She tells the drama troupe to go backstage and calls up the band.

As I walk onstage, even though I'm carrying my tuba in my arms, I feel like

I just swallowed it. We take our places, and Ms. Anderson raises her baton. With a swing of her arms, everyone begins.

The band starts to play the song we've been practicing for the last five weeks.

But something is wrong. When I blow, the sound that comes out doesn't sound the way it's supposed to. One of the clarinetists looks at me like I'm a zoo animal that wandered into the wrong exhibit. I feel like I don't belong here.

I keep blowing, but the sound that's coming out of my tuba doesn't at all match the notes on the page of music in front of me. Even though I played OK in rehearsal today, now that I'm onstage, I'm a bundle of nerves. I'm not sure all my practicing helped one bit.

When we're done playing the song, a lot of the band members are looking at me.

Ms. Anderson tells everyone to relax, but when she says it, she's looking at me. "Let's try that again," she says.

This time, I sound a little better, but I'm still off. "Maybe there is something wrong with my tuba," I say to Calvin.

Calvin gives me an *I'm-sorry-but-I-don't-think-anything-is-wrong-with-your-tuba* look. "I'm sure you'll get it right tomorrow night," he says.

I hope Calvin is right, but I'm not so sure.

Even though it wasn't perfect, Ms. Anderson doesn't ask us to do it again.

"There were a few hitches tonight," she says to the group. "But as I told you in rehearsal, that is what dress rehearsal is for."

Ms. Anderson is talking to the whole group, but I feel like the main person she's talking to is me. I feel like I'm the one who made the few hitches.

"Tomorrow night, I want you all to relax, have fun, and do your best," she says. "And I am sure you will be great."

Then she tells us all to go home and get a good night's sleep.

"I'm really nervous about tomorrow night," I tell Joey as we walk outside.

"You heard what Ms. Anderson said. "Just relax, have fun, and do your best."

"How did dress rehearsal go?" Mom asks as we get into the van.

"There were a few hitches," Joey tells her. "But I think we're ready for tomorrow night."

I buckle myself into my seat. I wish I felt as confident as Joey. I close my eyes and pretend like I'm at the wish pond on my street. I make a wish.

I wish the Spring Selections Showcase will go off without a hitch.

I keep my eyes closed for a long time.

I really, really, really want this wish to come true.

PRESHOW JITTERS

"Mallory, Max, time for dinner," Mom calls from the kitchen. "Hurry! We need to eat and leave for the show. We don't want to be late."

I button the top button on the white shirt that all the band members are wearing tonight. I look in the mirror. I might look like a musician, but I don't feel like one. As nervous as I was last night before dress rehearsal, that was nothing compared to how I feel now.

My knees are knocking. My throat is dry. My palms are sweaty. I don't feel ready.

I take one last look in the mirror. I don't know how Mom expects me to eat dinner tonight. Or play the tuba.

When I walk into the kitchen, I look at the plate of chicken and mashed potatoes sitting at my place at the table. Then I take a thermometer out of the cabinet and hand it to Mom. "I think you should take my temperature," I tell her. "I feel sick."

Mom sticks the thermometer into my mouth. "No fever," she says. Then she rubs my back. "Mallory, you're not sick. What you have are preshow jitters."

I frown. "That sounds bad. I can't go to the show." I slump in my chair. "It's probably contagious. I don't want other kids to get it."

Mom smiles. Then she explains that what I have is not contagious. "It is normal to be nervous before a performance. Once you get onstage and start playing, you will be fine."

My brother, Max, takes a bite of mashed potatoes. "I don't know about that. I heard her playing last night. Maybe you should let her stay home."

"Max!" Both my parents say my brother's name at the same time, and they don't say it in a very nice way.

"Everyone, eat your dinner, and then we're leaving," says Dad. "You have both been spending a lot of time practicing, and I am certain you will both perform beautifully."

I don't know how Dad can be so certain. He wasn't at the dress rehearsal last night.

We finish eating, grab my tuba and Max's drumsticks, and get into Mom's van.

When we get to school, the auditorium is already filling up with kids, teachers, and parents.

"Break a leg," Dad says and rumples my hair.

I know that's stage talk for "good luck." I'm going to need all the luck I can get.

Max and I head backstage. A lot of kids are already there. The band and orchestra members are wearing black pants and skirts and white shirts. The ballerinas are in pink. They have their hair pulled back into buns. The drama troupe is wearing their costumes.

"This is so exciting!" Mary Ann says when she arrives.

"I can't wait to play onstage!" says Joey.

Lots of kids look like they're excited. They're all talking and laughing like they don't have a care in the world. I don't see how they can feel so happy when I feel so nervous.

I spot Calvin holding his tuba. He's talking to one of the clarinetists and smiling. He looks like he's excited to go onstage too. At least half of the tuba section looks ready.

I peek from behind the curtain. The auditorium is filling up with people. Lots of them are holding video cameras.

I clutch my stomach. It feels like it's about to fall out of my body, through the floor, and to the other side of the world, which I think is China. Hopefully, whoever finds my stomach will return it.

Ms. Anderson comes over to where I'm standing and wraps an arm around me. "How are you doing, Mallory?"

I shake my head. I tell Ms. Anderson how nervous I am.

She nods like she understands. "That's normal," she says. Then she lowers her voice. "Try to relax. You've worked hard. You know what to do. Just focus on the piece of music that you're playing, and don't forget to breathe!" She smiles.

"I'll try," I tell Ms. Anderson.

"Places, everyone!" says Mrs. Denson.

All the Fern Falls fourth, fifth, and sixth graders start lining up behind the curtain for the opening number. Mrs. Denson, Mr. Michaels, Ms. Fontaine, and Ms. Anderson do a final check to make sure everyone is in the right spot.

Mrs. Denson gives the hand signal that

we are about to begin. Then she walks out onstage.

I close my eyes and repeat the wish I made in Mom's van last night.

I wish the Spring Selections Showcase will go off without a hitch.

I hear Mrs. Denson starting her welcome speech to the audience.

It's showtime!

REACHING FOR THE STARS

"Ladies and Gentlemen, welcome to the Fern Falls Elementary first ever Spring Selections Showcase."

Mrs. Denson waits while the audience claps.

I try to stand still in my place behind the curtain. But it's hard not to squirm knowing that the show starts as soon as Mrs. Denson finishes her introduction.

When the noise in the auditorium dies down, Mrs. Denson continues talking.

She explains to the audience how the fourth, fifth, and sixth graders have spent the last six weeks participating in ballet, drama, band, or orchestra. She tells them how hard everyone has worked to prepare for the show.

"The theme of tonight's performance is "Reaching for the Stars," says Mrs. Denson.

I look up at the ceiling of the stage. Even if Mrs. Denson hadn't told the audience the theme of the show, I think they would have figured it out. The ceiling is covered in little twinkling lights that look like stars. The front of the stage is decorated with cutouts of stars, and there are long, loopy paper chains of stars all over the auditorium.

I'm still nervous about performing, but I have to admit that it's exciting to see everything all lit up and decorated. Last night, when we came to the auditorium for dress rehearsal, it just looked like an auditorium. Tonight, it looks like a starry wonderland.

I listen as Mrs. Denson tells the audience to sit back and enjoy the show. The next thing I know, the curtain is rising. Grace, who is standing next to me, squeezes my hand. I squeeze back and look at her to see if she's nervous like I am. But she just looks excited.

As the curtain rises, the pianist onstage starts to play. Mrs. Denson motions for everyone to start singing "The Star-Spangled Banner."

I sing the words of the familiar song with the rest of the fourth, fifth, and sixth graders. I'm impressed with how loud and clear all our voices sound together.

When we finish singing, the audience claps. Their clapping is almost as loud as our singing. I can tell they really liked the performance.

I just hope the rest of the night goes as well as the opening number.

When the audience finishes clapping, everyone exits the stage like we practiced in dress rehearsal. I listen from backstage as Mr. Michaels calls the orchestra members to join him onstage. I can't see what they're doing, but I can hear chairs and music stands being moved around as they take their seats. Soon the sounds of "Catch a Falling Star" fill the auditorium.

I'm not an orchestra expert, but to me, they sound really good. Even though Pamela played the song for me on her violin, it didn't sound nearly as good as it does with the whole orchestra.

When they finish playing, the audience claps again.

I don't think there were any mistakes. I try to swallow, but it's hard. I hope the band sounds as good as the orchestra. Especially the tuba part of the band.

The next group to take the stage is the ballerinas. Ms. Fontaine introduces her dancers. I listen as the pianist starts to play their song, "Star Light, Star Bright."

When the music stops, there's more applause. Lots of it.

As the ballerinas come backstage, they're smiling and jumping around. I can tell they're happy with their performance.

I feel little beads of sweat forming on my forehead. I'm trying to stay relaxed, like Ms. Anderson told me to do, but it's not easy. So far, all the performances have been good. I take a deep breath.

I hear Mrs. Denson calling her drama troupe onstage. Their performance begins. I can hear them acting out a scene from *Pinocchio*. They finish by singing "When You Wish Upon a Star." Once again, the audience claps.

Part of me wants to play my tuba onstage. Part of me thinks I'm ready. I've worked hard and practiced for hours. But another part of me would like to take the first bus out of town. I'm just not sure I can do this.

As the drama troupe returns backstage, Ms. Anderson motions for the band members to line up. It's time to go onstage. I pick up my tuba and my music and get in line. Ms. Anderson leads us onto the stage. I position my chair. I lay my music carefully on my stand.

When I look out at the auditorium full of people, my stomach starts to rumble. It's almost as loud as my tuba. I look around to see if anyone heard, but no one seems to be paying attention to me. People are busy getting their own instruments and music ready for the performance.

I take a deep breath. I make the same wish I made last night, one more time just to be safe. I cross my toes and squeeze my eyes shut. *I wish Spring Selections Showcase will go off without a hitch.*

But I don't keep my eyes shut for long.

Ms. Anderson introduces the band. Then she turns to us and raises her baton. We lift our instruments into playing position.

It's performance time!

I focus on the music. I make my brain go back over all the tricks Ms. Anderson taught me to sound better when I play.

I look down at the sheet music on the stand in front of me. I raise my tuba to my mouth and start to blow. Sounds of the band playing "Twinkle, Twinkle, Little Star" fill the auditorium.

I keep blowing into my mouthpiece as my lips buzz. So far, so good.

I breathe out from deep in my belly, like Ms. Anderson taught me. The sound that comes out of my tuba is clear and low, just like it should be.

I press valves as my fingers find their way into the right combinations.

I focus on the notes in front of me. I make sure to watch Ms. Anderson's baton out of the corner of my eye so I don't start going faster than everyone else.

Before I know it, I'm on the last note. I look up to see when Ms. Anderson cuts off the band.

The room is silent for just a second, and then the audience is clapping and cheering. I look out at the auditorium. Lots of people are even standing up and clapping.

I did it! I, Mallory McDonald, played "Twinkle, Twinkle, Little Star," and I played it without a hitch. My wish came true. I even got a standing ovation.

I don't know how rock stars feel after a concert, but I know I feel great. I look down at my tuba. I know what Ms. Anderson meant when she talked about music magic. I feel it right now.

Ms. Anderson asks the band members to stand. We do. Then we bow to the audience just like she taught us to do.

Mrs. Denson, Mr. Michaels, and Ms. Fontaine lead their performers onstage to join the band members. When all the performers are onstage, the audience stands up and claps even harder.

Mrs. Denson thanks everyone for coming. Then she motions to everyone onstage. "I don't think there are brighter stars anywhere," she says. Then she claps for us herself.

Soon the curtain falls.

Spring Selections is over, but the applause keeps going.

THE AFTER PARTY

The show was a big hit, and by the looks of things, the after party is going to be too.

The lobby outside the Fern Falls Elementary School auditorium is standing room only. There are musicians, dancers, performers, parents, and best of all . . . cookies and punch!

Everyone is laughing and talking.

Joey grabs my arm. "Great job!" he says. "Now it's time to eat!"

I don't know if it's because I didn't eat dinner or just the excitement from the show, but suddenly, I'm starving. I follow Joey to the cookie table, but before we get there, Mrs. Finney starts to talk into the microphone.

"May I have your attention, please," she says.

Everyone stops talking.

"I want to congratulate all of you on a wonderful show. You did a magnificent job." She claps and parents clap along with her. Then everyone starts cheering.

Mrs. Finney waits for the noise to die down. "I'd like to take a moment to recognize some very special people." She calls Mrs. Denson, Mr. Michaels, Ms. Fontaine, and Ms. Anderson to join her.

When they do, she smiles at all of them. "Spring Selections was a tremendous success. We couldn't have done it without your leadership, talent, and guidance. I'd like to thank each one of you on behalf of all the students and parents of Fern Falls Elementary." Mrs. Finney has four bouquets of roses, and she gives one to each of the directors.

When she finishes, there is a lot more applause, whistling, and cheering.

Mrs. Finney smiles and waits like she has something else she wants to say. But this time, she has to wait a very long time for the noise to die down. It's easy to see that everyone loved Spring Selections and really appreciated all the directors.

After a few minutes, Mrs. Finney taps on her microphone. "I want to add one last thing."

Everyone gets quiet as we wait to hear what Mrs. Finney has to say. She has a look on her face like what she's going to say is very serious, but then her face changes. She breaks out into a big smile and raises one arm in the air. "It's party time!" she yells into the microphone.

The room fills with cheers.

I look around for my friends. But before I have a chance to find them, someone finds me, and that someone is Ms. Anderson.

When she sees me,
she wraps her
arm around
my shoulder.

"Mallory,
I'm so proud
of you!
You played
beautifully."
Then she gives
me an *all-your-practice-paid-off* look. "I knew
you could do it."

I smile. "Thanks! It was actually a lot of
fun! I think now I know what you mean by
music magic."

"I'm just happy it all worked out," says
Ms. Anderson.

There's one more thing I want to say.
"Ms. Anderson, I couldn't have done it
without you. Thanks for all your help."

Ms. Anderson looks down at me. It almost looks like she has tears in her eyes. She gives me a big hug. "Thank you, Mallory. There's nothing you could have said that could make me any happier." I watch as Ms. Anderson walks off and starts talking to another student.

I didn't think I would ever have fun playing the tuba, but tonight, when I hit the right notes, I had a really good time doing what I was doing.

I walk back into the auditorium and look at the stage. All the stars look so pretty hanging from the ceiling. It's like the whole auditorium is twinkling.

Mom and Dad find me while I'm still stargazing. Max is with them. Mom gives me a big hug. "We're so proud of our tuba player," she says.

"I couldn't agree more," says Dad.

Then he makes Max and me pose together for a picture.

I put one hand on my hip and give Dad a big smile. Max sticks around for a few photos and then says he has to find Dylan. "We're going to start a band."

Mom smiles when he says that.

Mom and Dad and I go back to where the party is. Joey and Mary Ann find me. They already have cookies and punch. Joey hands me a cup of punch, and Mary Ann has a plate piled high with cookies for me.

"Cheers!" says Joey.

"Cheers!" Mary Ann and I say at the same time.

We all three clink our cups of punch together.

Some nights are good. Some nights are great. Some nights are a celebration.

And tonight is one of those nights.

THE AFTER-
AFTER PARTY

The after party was fun. But the after-after party is going to be awesome.

"Hurry up!" I tell Mary Ann.

Mary Ann throws her pillow at me. I catch it just before it bops me on the head. She laughs. "I just need to change into my pj's, and then I'm ready," she says.

When she's done, we climb out her window, walk from her yard to mine, and

climb in my window. When we're in my
room, I slip on my musical note pajamas.
Mary Ann is wearing pajamas with little
ballerinas on them. Usually we match, but
tonight, things are a little different.

"Let the after-after party begin!" I
shout.

Mary Ann and I fall on my bed laughing.
I grab Cheeseburger, and she rolls around
on my bed with us. It has been a long day,
but not the kind of long day that makes
you sleepy. It has been the kind of day that
makes you feel wide awake, which is good,
because for our after-after party, Mary Ann
and I are planning an all-night stay-awake-
over.

It's like a sleepover, but instead of
sleeping, you stay awake. Mary Ann and
I have never done it before, but tonight,
we're determined to stay up all night.

We came up with the idea at the after party. It just seemed so sad when the lobby was emptying out and the party was coming to an end. Mary Ann and I both wanted to keep things going, so we are.

I pull out my clipboard and a purple marker. "Let's make a schedule," I say.

"We could start with snacks and TV," says Mary Ann.

I frown. "We need to start our stay-awake-over with something more exciting than that." I scratch my head to help me think. Then I snap my fingers. "I have a great idea! Why don't we start with performances."

Mary Ann makes an *I'm-not-sure-what-you-mean* face. So I explain. "Since I was backstage when you danced, why don't you do your dance so I can see it. And since you were backstage when the band played our piece, I will play it for you."

Mary Ann grins like she loves that idea. "We have everything we need. You have your tuba, and I have a CD of the music I danced to."

I'm glad Mary Ann likes my idea. I was so nervous tonight while I was waiting for my turn to play onstage, but now that I know I can perform my piece without any mistakes, I would love to play it again. Dad opens the door to my room. "How are the performers doing?" he asks.

Now it's my turn to grin. There's only one thing Mary Ann and I need to make our solo performances even more fun, and that's an audience. "Hey, Dad. Mary Ann and I were just about to perform our pieces from the show. Would you and Mom like to watch?"

Dad smiles. "We would love it.

"Give us five minutes, and we'll meet you in the living room," I tell Dad.

When we get to the living room, Mom and Dad are sitting on the couch. Even Max is there, and he has his dog, Champ, with him. I run back down the hall and pick up Cheeseburger, who is asleep on my bed. I put her on the couch next to Champ. Now we have a real audience.

"A private performance!" says Mom as I pull up a chair to perform first. "Play it again, Mallory!"

Everyone claps. I think of all the times Ms. Anderson said those same words to

me and how much I hated hearing them.
I never thought I would say this, but I'm
excited to play my piece again.

I bow to my audience and then take
my seat. I raise my tuba to my lips. I start
to blow and push valves on my tuba. Big,
deep, clear sounds of "Twinkle, Twinkle,
Little Star" fill our living room. When I'm
done, I bow again, and everyone claps.

This time, I didn't feel nervous as I played.
I felt confident. I knew the notes, and I
played them all right. I grin at my audience.

My solo performance felt fantastic.

"Good job, Mallory!" says Mom.

"I'm blown away," says Dad. Then he laughs. "Just a little tuba humor."

Even Max claps and smiles like he enjoyed the performance.

I'm glad my brother liked the way I played. "Hey, Max, maybe I can play in your band."

Max stops smiling. "Sorry, Mal. I don't think we need a tuba player."

I shrug. "If you change your mind, you know where to find me."

Everyone laughs. I squeeze onto the couch between Champ and Cheeseburger. Mary Ann gets up and turns on her CD. Soon the sounds of "Star Light, Star Bright" fill the room.

Mary Ann turns and twirls and dips and spins.

I always knew she was good at hip-hop. But I didn't realize she would be so good at ballet. When the song is done, she curtsies to the audience.

We all clap. Dad puts his fingers in his mouth and lets out a loud whistle. We all stand up and keep clapping to show Mary Ann how much we liked her dance.

"Two stellar performances!" says Dad.

Mom nods like she agrees. "Are either of the performers hungry?" asks Mom.

"I don't know if they are, but I am," says Max.

"Me too," says Dad.

Mary Ann and I both nod. I didn't know playing an instrument could make you so hungry. We all follow Mom into the kitchen. She starts pulling containers out of the refrigerator. Spaghetti and meatballs. Leftover chicken. Cut-up fruit.

Lemonade. Dad takes graham crackers, marshmallows, and chocolate bars out of a cabinet.

"This is going to be a feast!" I say.

We all pull up chairs and start putting food on plates.

I eat a big plate of spaghetti and meatballs. Mary Ann makes an oversized s'more. Mom has a plate of fruit, and Dad eats some chicken. Max eats some of everything.

I push my plate back when I'm done. "I'm stuffed," I say.

"Me too," says Mary Ann.

Even Max pats his stomach like he couldn't put anything else in it.

"I'm sure everyone is full and tired," says Mom. She gives Mary Ann and me kisses on the head. "Why don't you girls brush up and get in bed."

"OK," I tell Mom. Then I wink at Mary Ann. We're not planning to tell Mom and Dad about our stay-awake-over. One thing I know for sure is that they would not approve of our plan.

When Mary Ann and I get back to my room, I get my clipboard and marker. "OK," I say to Mary Ann. "Planning Time. I look at my clock. It's only 10:45. We need to make a plan for every hour."

Mary Ann and I start planning and writing.

☆ Mallory AND Mary Ann's ☆
Stay-Awake-over Schedule.
☆ 11:00 Toenail Painting
☆ 12:00 Make Friendship Bracelets ☆
1:00 Tell Scary Stories
2:00 Read Joke Books ☆
3:00 Sneak into Kitchen for Snacks
☆ 4:00 Truth or Dare
☆ 5:00 Makeovers ☆
6:00 Look at Old Scrapbooks
☆ 7:00 Watch Cartoons ☆ ☆
8:00 Eat Pancakes!!!! ☆ ☆

When we finish planning, Mary Ann and I look at each other. Mary Ann yawns. I rub my eyes. I don't know if it was our solo performances, our after-after party feast, or all of our planning, but all of a sudden, I feel sleepy.

I look at my clock. It's 10:55. "We still have five minutes before it's time to start painting our toenails," I say to Mary Ann.

"Why don't we just lie down on my bed until eleven."

"Good idea," says Mary Ann in a sleepy voice.

I put my head on my pillow. Mary Ann lays her head on my other pillow.

"Maybe you should turn the light out while we rest," says Mary Ann.

"Right," I say again. But my voice sounds farther away this time.

I roll over and turn out my light.

"Just five minutes," I hear Mary Ann's voice in the dark.

"Just five minutes," is the last thing I remember saying before I fall fast asleep.

A SHINING STAR

"Boys and girls, it's time to turn in your instruments."

Ms. Anderson's band room fills with groans and boos and hisses. It's clear that lots of kids are sad Spring Selections is over and that they don't want to turn in their instruments. I never thought I'd say this, but I, Mallory McDonald, am officially one of those kids.

I do NOT want to give back my tuba!

Ms. Anderson asks all of us to place our instruments against the back wall. Then she goes down the line of instruments making little checks on a clipboard. "All the instruments are in good shape," she announces when she's done.

If she's expecting everyone to cheer, she's going to be disappointed. No one looks too happy. Ms. Anderson smiles. "I hope all of these long faces are a sign that you enjoyed being in the band."

We all clap to show her that we did. Max and his friend, Dylan, let out a loud whistle.

Ms. Anderson smiles and bows. "I'm thrilled you all enjoyed your experience in the band, and I hope it is something many of you will pursue in middle school." Ms. Anderson raises a finger like she's about to make an important point.

"The fun here hasn't quite come to an end. I still have a few surprises in store." She reaches behind the desk and pulls out a shopping bag. "Time for awards and prizes!" she says.

I look at the bag in her hand. I silently wish that one of those awards has my name on it, even though I don't think it's going to.

Ms. Anderson gives out the award for Most Improved to Pete. He definitely deserves it. I remember his cymbal playing the first week. It sounded like someone dropped a stack of dishes. He really has improved so much from when he first started.

Everyone claps when she hands him his ribbon.

The next award is for Musical Excellence. It goes to a fifth-grade girl named Jamie who played the flute. "A truly fine flutist." Ms. Anderson gives Jamie a big hug when she goes up to accept her award.

There's more clapping.

The award for A+ Attitude goes to C-Lo. "One of the quickest learners and nicest trombone players I have ever had the privilege of teaching," Ms. Anderson says as she hands C-Lo his award.

He thanks Ms. Anderson and then waves his certificate in the air and grins like he's really happy. The room fills with claps and cheers and even a few whistles.

As happy as I am for Pete and Jamie and C-Lo, I cross my toes that one of the remaining awards in her bag has the name Mallory McDonald written on it.

Ms. Anderson takes the next award from the bag. "This award is for the Most Enthusiastic Musician. I am giving it to two musicians who played the drums and who I hear have plans to start their own band." She smiles in my brother and his friend's direction. "Max and Dylan, will you please come up to accept your awards."

My brother has a huge smile on his face, and so does Dylan. They hold their awards up like they're posing for a photo op. They

haven't even started a band, and they're
already acting like they're rock stars.

Everyone claps and cheers, and I do too.

"Now for the last award," says Ms.
Anderson.

I uncross my toes. I don't think any
amount of toe crossing is going to help me
win an award at this point.

"The last award I'm giving out today is called the Shining Star award. It goes to the students who got every answer correct on the music quiz that I gave. There were four students who won this award. Please come up as I call out your names."

I recross my toes. Maybe I do have a chance.

"Grace Reyes."

My friend and classmate crosses the room to accept her award.

One down, three more to go. I cross my toes even tighter.

"Olivia Fine."

I watch as Arielle's older sister accepts her award. This isn't good. Only two more awards. My toes are starting to ache.

"Brett Jones."

I take a deep breath as Max's friend crosses the room to get his award. There's only one award left. Even though they hurt, I cross my toes as tightly as I've ever crossed them.

I watch as Ms. Anderson reaches into her bag for what I know will be the last time.

Please let it be me.

"Mallory McDonald." Ms. Anderson smiles as she says my name.

I spring out of my seat. I'm at the front of the room in no time. "Thanks!" I say to Ms. Anderson. I give her a big hug.

She smiles at me. "You earned it, Mallory."

Everyone claps as I sit down.

When the bell rings, everyone leaves the room single file as Ms. Anderson hands out Certificates of Participation to everyone in the band.

I get in the back of the line. There's one last thing I want to say to Ms. Anderson before I leave.

I clear my throat as she hands me my certificate. "Ms. Anderson, I just wanted to say thanks again for the pep talk and for helping me so much."

Ms. Anderson smiles. "Mallory, it was a pleasure watching you develop into a real tuba player and a shining star." She wraps an arm around my shoulders. "I really hope you will consider joining the band when you get to middle school."

I nod my head like I will definitely consider it. I never thought I would be saying this, but I, Mallory McDonald, think making music is a lot of fun.

A SCRAPBOOK

Spring Selections Showcase turned out to be an awesome night. It was really fun playing the tuba and being part of the band. The audience definitely enjoyed the show. And I know everyone enjoyed the after party! Mom took lots of pictures. So of course, Mary Ann and I made a scrapbook. I think it's one of our best ever! We put in photos from the songs that were showcased.

We're going to take it to school tomorrow to show to our friends, but we wanted to give you a sneak peek of some of our favorite pages.

Here's the page with everyone singing
"The Star-Spangled Banner."

the star-spangled Banner

BY Francis Scott Key

O say can you see,
by the dawn's early light,
What so proudly we hail'd
at the twilight's last gleaming,
Whose broad stripes
and bright stars
through the perilous fight,
O'er the ramparts we watch'd,
were so gallantly streaming?
And the rockets red glare,
the bombs bursting in air,
Gave proof through the night
that our flag was still there,
O say does that star-spangled
banner yet wave
O'er the land of the free
and the home of the brave?

Spring Selections

Here's the orchestra page. They're
playing "Catch a Falling Star."

Here's the ballet page. Mary Ann looked
great dancing to "Star Light, Star Bright" in
her starry outfit!

Here's the drama group singing "When You Wish Upon a Star."

And here's the band playing "Twinkle, Twinkle, Little Star"!

There are lots more pages, but our favorite page is the after-party page!

We hope you have as much fun looking at our scrapbook as we had making it!

A MUSIC QUIZ

If you don't play a musical instrument,
you can still be a music star. Just try taking
the same quiz I took. If you don't know
an answer, all you have to do is turn the
page and sneak a peek! Not only did I
give you the answers, but I added my own
explanations as well.

Directions: choose A, B, C, or D for the correct musical
definition of each word.

1. A CAPPELLA

A. a small hat
B. a large hat
C. a furry animal
D. singing without instruments

2. BASS

A. the lowest sounds
B. the highest sounds
C. a brand of shoes
D. a type of fish

3. CHORD

A. a piece of string

B. a line between two points

C. three or more notes played at the same time.

D. an emotional response

4. KEY

A. something used to open a door

B. the answer to a problem

C. notes of a song centered on a certain note or class

D. part of a basketball court

5. SOLO

A. a type of cup

B. song played by a single instrument

C. all alone

D. not high up

6. TEMPO

A. timing or speed of the music

B. a secretary in an office

C. pasta with tomatoes

D. an Argentinean dance

7. DOLCE

A. a type of ice cream
B. cookies with nuts
C. ladies who sing in church
D. a sweet style of playing music

8. FORTE

A. a protective house
B. a wall of logs
C. a big hammer
D. a loud or strong style of music

9. STANZA

A. not sitting down
B. the verse of a song
C. a type of tool
D. another name for the flu

10. SCORE

A. the written version of music
B. points in a game
C. finger pointing
D. finger painting

THE ANSWERS

By Mallory McDonald

1. **D. A Cappella** is an Italian word that describes music that is sung without accompanying instruments. Definitely not a hat (small or large) or a furry animal!

2. **A. Bass** (pronounced "base," as in first, second, or third) describes musical instruments that make low-pitched sounds, like my tuba. There are fish called bass. Dad says they are fun to catch. Mom says they taste delicious. I would rather eat ice cream.

3. **C. Chord.** A chord is three or more notes played at the same time. A chord can also be a piece of string, a line between two points, or an emotional response. But none of those definitions have anything to do with music!

4. **C. Key.** Here is Ms. Anderson's definition: A key is the major or minor scale around which a piece of music revolves. I'm still not 100% sure what this means, but I know it's important when you're talking about music (and opening front doors).

5. **B. Solo.** This is a piece of music played by a single instrument or a song sung by a single person. Here it is used in a sentence: I liked playing a solo at the after-

after party. I would not have wanted to play one at the showcase!

6. **A. Tempo.** Time or speed of the music. Not a secretary. Not pasta. Not a dance.

7. **D. Dolce.** An Italian word pronounced Dolch-A (rhymes with stay or play). It means sweet in Italian. So when you're talking about music, it means playing it sweetly.

8. **D. Forte.** It sounds like something you build with your friends in the backyard. In musical terms, playing forte means to play with strength or loudly (a good idea if you want to keep your brother out of your room while you're playing).

9. **B. Stanza.** The verse of a song. There are lots of famous songs with lots of famous stanzas. If you can't think of any (which I know you will be able to), Google it!

10. **A. Score.** The written-down version of music. To put it in simple terms, it's a piece of paper that tells all the instruments what to do. Of course, it is also points in a game or points on a test, which if you took this one, I give you 10 out of 10! That's an A+! Perfect! Wow!

YOU ARE A MUSIC SUPERSTAR!

Darby Creek
A division of Lerner Publishing Group, Inc.
241 First Avenue North
Minneapolis, MN 55401 U.S.A.

Website address: www.lernerbooks.com

Cover background: © iStockphoto.com/Jayesh.

Main body text set in LuMarcLL 14/20. Typeface provided by Linotype.

Library of Congress Cataloging-in-Publication Data

Friedman, Laurie B., 1964-
    Play it again, Mallory / by Laurie Friedman ; illustrations by Jennifer Kalis.
       p.   cm. — (Mallory ; #20)
    ISBN 978-0-7613-6075-9 (trade hard cover : alk. paper)
    ISBN 978-1-4677-1621-5 (eBook)
    [1. Bands (Music)—Fiction. 2. Music—Fiction. 3. Schools—Fiction.] I. Kalis,
Jennifer, illustrator. II. Title.
PZ7.F89773Pl 2013
[Fic]—dc23   2012048866

Manufactured in the United States of America
1 — BP — 7/15/13